BONK!

Way Beyond Therapy

by

SCHULZ

CollinsPublishersSanFrancisco
A Division of HarperCollins*Publishers*

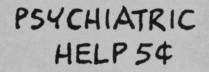

That'll Be 5¢, Please

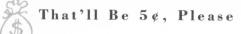 **That'll Be 5¢, Please**

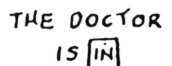

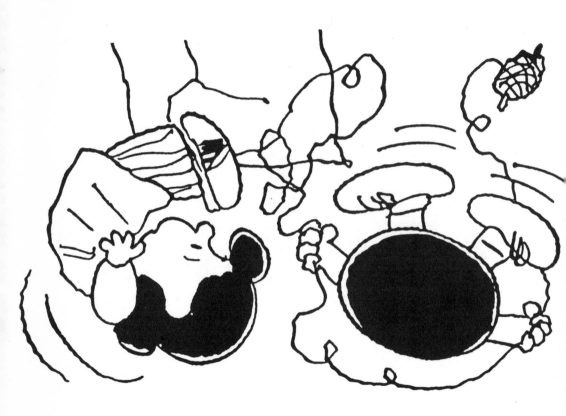

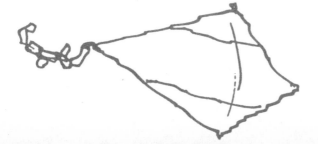

MATURITY IS WHAT YOU SHOULD STRIVE FOR, CHARLIE BROWN...

THE DOCTOR

A MATURE PERSON IS A PATIENT PERSON... SOMEBODY WHO DOESN'T DEMAND EVERYTHING **NOW**!

THE DOCTOR

THAT'S GOOD TO KNOW BECAUSE I CAN'T PAY YOU UNTIL TOMORROW...

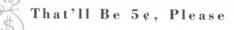

That'll Be 5¢, Please

Just Testing

Medicine Worse Than The Malady

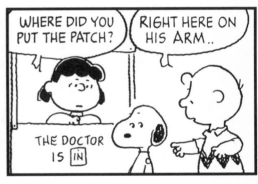

Medicine Worse Than The Malady

Driving
On The Freeway
Of Life

THIS PART
IS MY
FAVORITE

Maybe You're Normal

OPINIONS - 5¢

THOUGHTS FOR
THE DAY - 10¢

SOUND ADVICE - 25¢

Advice To Laugh By

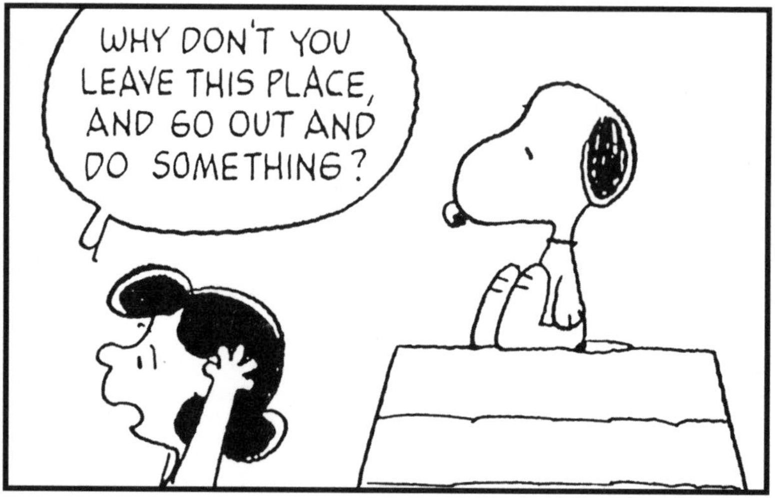
WHY DON'T YOU LEAVE THIS PLACE, AND GO OUT AND DO SOMETHING?

SHE ALWAYS SAYS,"LAUGH BEFORE SUPPER, CRY BEFORE BED"

THE DOCTOR IS IN

WHAT DO YOU THINK I SHOULD DO?

THE DOCTOR IS IN

A Packaged Goods Incorporated Book
First published 1996 by Collins Publishers San Francisco
1160 Battery Street, San Francisco, CA 94111-1213
http://www.harpercollins.com
Conceived and produced by Packaged Goods Incorporated
276 Fifth Avenue, New York, NY 10001
A Quarto Company

Library of Congress Cataloging-in-Publication Data
Schulz, Charles M.
[Peanuts. Selections]
Way beyond therapy / by Schulz.
p.   cm.
ISBN 0-00-225193-0
I. Title
PN6728.P4S345   1996
741.5'973—dc20   96-15796
                      CIP

Printed in Hong Kong

1 3 5 7 9 10 8 6 4 2